MAGIC

Gem

Atl
Adventure

Written by De-ann Black
Illustrated by Derick Bown

HENDERSON
PUBLISHING LTD

©1997 HENDERSON PUBLISHING LTD

©1997 Henderson Publishing Ltd

*All rights reserved.
This paperback is sold subject to the condition
that it shall not, by way of trade or otherwise, be lent, resold, hired
out, or otherwise circulated in any form of binding or cover, or by any
other means, electronic, mechanical, recording, or otherwise, without
the prior written permission of Henderson Publishing Ltd.*

Contents

1	The Crystal Cavern	5
2	Pico and the Pool of Destiny	17
3	The Tunnel of Fear	31
4	Flores and the Sapphire Lake	48
5	The Flames of Wrath	60
6	The Gem Star	73
7	Pico Sees Clearly	86

1. The Crystal Cavern

Gemma peered out of the plane window at the islands below. "Look, Dad, there's Atlantis!" she said excitedly. Nine small islands floated like precious jewels in the sparkling turquoise waters of the Atlantic Ocean.

"It's the Azores, Gemma," her dad corrected. "Atlantis is just a myth. No one knows for sure whether it even existed."

"*I* believe it existed," said Gemma confidently. "I've read all about it. Atlantis disappeared into the sea thousands of years ago, after volcanoes erupted and destroyed the whole civilisation. The Azores are supposed to have formed part of the sunken continent which is lost forever in the depths of the sea."

Jim James gave his daughter a doubtful smile. "Legends are very nice, but without scientific proof they're nothing more than fantastic stories."

Gemma darted an offended look at him.

"Some things are impossible to prove, but surely they can still be true? History is full of unexplained mysteries and deep, dark secrets."

She imagined her dad's reaction if he ever found out about her magic jewellery. What scientific explanation would he give for her amazing adventures through time? He was always so frustratingly logical, believing in nothing but fact. If it wasn't carved in stone with accuracy guaranteed, he wouldn't accept it. Dad had the ultimate logical mind – perhaps that was why he was such a good diplomat.

She folded her arms. "Anyway, I think Atlantis must have been a wonderful place – just like paradise."

Turning her head, she gazed out at the rainbow-coloured scenery as the plane approached its destination.

Blue and green lagoons nestled between sleeping volcanic craters. A patchwork of lush, green countryside dotted with whitewashed houses spread out beneath them, and even from this height Gemma could see flowers sprinkled over the landscape like multicoloured sweets.

For the next four days they were staying on the largest island. Dad was here on business and, after some persistent persuasion, he had agreed to take Gemma with him. He made these trips two or three times a year, always promising one day to take her along. Well, thought Gemma contentedly to herself, this time he's kept his promise!

As they landed on São Miguel, she could hardly contain her excitement. The sun shone brightly in an endless blue sky, and the view from her hotel room was breathtaking. Bay windows opened out on to a veranda, its ornate railings entwined with exotic flowers. Their fragrance wafted in on a tranquil sea breeze, which puffed up the brightly-coloured sails of distant boats bobbing on the gentle waves. A ribbon of golden beach fringed the coast, and the reflection of the painted houses was mirrored in the clear turquoise sea.

Gemma could hardly wait to go

exploring, but she had promised Dad that she would stay in the hotel until he returned from his business meeting. These meetings, he had said, were usually over in two or three hours, and she should expect him back some time in the afternoon.

Afterwards, he said that he would take her swimming in the Twin Lakes, and Gemma couldn't wait.

From her window, she could see the lakes shimmering invitingly in the midday sun. This made her even more restless. "Oh well," she reasoned, "I'm sure exploring the hotel is allowed."

Venturing downstairs, she decided to visit the shops in the hotel reception. The jeweller's shop caught her eye, and she stopped to look at the glittering necklaces displayed in the window.

Milky-white pearls shone with a translucent glow, alongside gleaming silver beads, diamond-cut rubies, and sparkling sapphires blue as a midnight ocean.

A sign claimed that the necklaces were of a traditional design and handcrafted in the Azores.

What a coincidence, Gemma thought, gazing at the delicate, diamond-shaped beads in red, white, blue and silver. She had a necklace very similar to these! Perhaps it too came from the Azores. Or maybe...just maybe, it came from Atlantis.

Wandering into the shop, a lady smiled at her from behind the counter. "Can I help you?"

"I'm just browsing, if that's okay," said Gemma cheerfully.

"Oh yes, you're welcome," said the woman, speaking impeccable English with a Portuguese accent.

"Your necklaces are beautiful," said Gemma.

"Thank you. Each piece is specially crafted in the Azores."

"The sign says the designs are traditional," remarked Gemma, studying the beads closely.

"That's right. The patterns are ancient, passed down through the centuries."

"Would this be the type of necklace worn in Atlantis?" asked Gemma, her curiosity getting the better of her.

The woman laughed lightly. "So, you believe in the legend of the lost continent, do you?"

"Oh yes, don't you?"

"Of course, but some people think it's just a myth."

"My dad's one of them. He thinks it's nonsense, but then he would. He doesn't believe in anything mystical or magical."

"Is your father here with you in the Azores?"

"Yes," Gemma replied.

The lady looked wistful. "This island is

full of unexplained mysteries and strange happenings." She paused, then made a suggestion. "If you like myths and legends, you should ask your father to take you to the Lake of Fire. It's a fascinating place."

"Where is it?"

"Oh, not far from the town. Anyone will give your father directions, but you must go before dark so that you can see the fire appear at nightfall."

Gemma couldn't believe her ears. "Do you mean that the water is really on fire?"

"You'd have to decide that for yourself. The lake is set within the crater of an ancient volcano that has been dormant for years. During the day the water is clear, but at night it has a distinctive fiery-red glow."

"What makes the water glow?"

The woman shrugged. "No one knows. Legend has it that it's the everlasting flame of Atlantis – a reminder that the past is forever a part of the future."

"Oh yes," said Gemma eagerly. She knew this already, having travelled back and forth through time with her magic jewellery.

She looked again at the jewels in front of her.

"I've got a necklace very similar to these," she said thoughtfully, almost to herself, mentally comparing them to the one which she had in her jewellery box.

The woman seemed surprised. "It must have originated in the Azores."

"Perhaps it even came from Atlantis!" said Gemma.

"Well, you never know. These designs are copies of ones so ancient that the original designs are difficult to trace. But we do know the mythical meaning of the beads."

"What do you mean – the mythical meaning?"

The woman pointed to a white card printed with small gold lettering which was sitting on top of a display case. Gemma read the words aloud.

"True love shines in the crimson light.
Blue reflects the secrets of the sea.
Silver mirrors the moon at night.
Pearls stand for truth and purity."

"If you have your necklace with you, you should wear it in the Azores for good luck," the woman suggested.

"Hmmm, I might just do that. Thank you for taking the time to tell me all about the jewellery – it's been really interesting," replied Gemma gratefully.

The woman smiled.

As she left the shop, Gemma could hardly contain her excitement. She had every intention of wearing her necklace – but not just for luck!

She hurried up the hotel stairs to her room. Pulling out her suitcase, which she still hadn't bothered to unpack, she rummaged impatiently for her jewellery box which was hidden carefully beneath her clothes.

Lifting it out on to the bed, she opened the lid to reveal the familiar tangle of necklaces, earrings and bracelets.

The deep red and blue droplets of the necklace which she was looking for shone through the other strands of assorted beads and trinkets. Carefully, she retrieved it and shook it free. Looking at it, she remembered the day she had found the magic necklaces hidden in the cave on the beach in Cornwall, where she had been staying with her uncle. That strange discovery had changed her life forever! These necklaces were special – mysteriously magical. Like some ancient puzzle, Gemma had read the piece of yellowed parchment which was stowed away with them, and had unravelled something so fantastic, so utterly incredible, that she hadn't told a soul. Besides, she had reasoned with herself, no one would believe her if she told them that the necklaces gave her the ability to travel through time – and who could blame them? Holding the necklace up to the sunlight, she gazed through the clear crimson beads which dangled in the middle, admiring the fire-like flames flickering in their depths. 'You should wear it in the Azores for good luck.' The words of the jeweller whispered temptingly in her mind.

Hastily, Gemma debated with herself. Maybe this necklace would have the power to take her back in time to the lost continent of Atlantis – the magic had worked before, but dare she go? She'd read about Atlantis being engulfed by a volcanic disaster, so how could she guarantee that her necklace wouldn't land her right in the middle of it? She toyed distractedly with the beads, watching them twinkle in the sunlight.

Well, she thought, making up her mind – there's only one way to find out!

Undoing the clasp, she draped the magic beads around her neck and whispered to herself, "Take me to the lost continent of Atlantis..."

Taking a deep breath, she fastened the clasp securely. The room turned in a wild, swirling blur and vanished. Gemma could hear a voice in her head, chanting,

*You shall journey far and wide
Across Time's endless seas...*

And as the voice chanted, Gemma felt herself falling down, down, down, down...

All around her dazzling flashes of blue

and green light sparkled, causing Gemma to blink uncertainly at their brilliance.

As her eyes grew accustomed to the strange light, she looked around and found herself standing inside a beautiful crystal cavern. Water, the colour of aquamarine, flowed down one side of the cavern, casting everything in a greeny-blue glow. The cold, clean air made her nostrils twitch. As she realised where she was, Gemma's tummy did a somersault.

"Atlantis!" she whispered, as she stood in awe of her otherworldly surroundings. "It does exist – it's real!"

"Of course it's real," said a voice.

Gemma spun around, and jumped to see a man sitting in a corner of the cavern. He looked very old. His hair was silvery-white and he was wearing long, flowing, turquoise robes. As Gemma stared at him, intelligent, pale blue eyes stared right back at her in astonishment.

"Who are you?" she gasped, and then kicked herself for being so blunt.

"Who are *you*?" the man countered, his powerful voice echoing around the cavern.

Gemma shifted awkwardly from foot to foot. Now what do I do, she thought to herself nervously. I've got to think of something to say – but what?

2. Pico and the Pool of Destiny

Darting furtive glances around the cavern, Gemma approached the old man. He was sitting in a chair which reminded her of the pictures in old fairy tale books Mum had given her to read when she was little. It was carved out of wood and inset with decorative, turquoise stones. The old man's long, flowing robes rippled like watered silk, and around his neck he wore a silver moon-shaped pendant.

Beside his chair, Gemma could see a small pool which seemed to be carved into the crystal cavern. Vivid blue-green water shimmered like a mirror in the middle, and scalloped seashells encrusted with multi-coloured gemstones dappled the outer edges. Wow! thought Gemma. The beauty of the place took her breath away.

The old man studied her thoughtfully. Self-consciously, Gemma noticed that he kept looking at her necklace, as if the design meant something to him. Perhaps the lady in the jeweller's had been right after all!

"You have nothing to fear from me," he said gently, dissolving the silence between them.

"Who are you?" Gemma whispered, encouraged by his friendly manner.

"My name is Pico," he replied. "I am the seer of Atlantis."

"What's a seer?"

"You *are* curious!" replied Pico, quietly amused by her outspoken manner. "A seer is someone who can see into the future. Does that answer your question?"

Gemma blushed and nodded.

"And now I think it's fair for me to ask you your name," he added.

"I'm Gemma – Gemma James," she answered, a little apprehensively.

He smiled at her. "So, Gemma James,

what are you doing in Atlantis?"

She hesitated – should she tell him? A wise and mystical man like him would surely understand better than anyone else. He waited patiently for her reply.

"Well, I'm not sure whether you'll believe me or not," she said doubtfully.

He sat back in his chair and watched her. "If you tell me the truth, I'll believe you."

Something about the way he spoke to her encouraged Gemma to confide in him. "I'm from the future," she began. "I'd always dreamed of visiting Atlantis, and I used my magic jewellery to bring me here."

"The future?"

"Yes, I don't know how far back in time I've travelled, but it's at least a thousand years, perhaps two thousand..."

"Remarkable!" he gasped.

She fiddled nervously with her necklace as she continued to explain. "These beads belong to my magic jewellery collection. By wearing the necklaces, I can travel back in time to anywhere in the world. I've had all sorts of exciting adventures already – but Atlantis is a dream come true!"

19

"Your beads are certainly of Atlantean design," he observed.

"So you believe me?" she asked hopefully.

"I think you are telling the truth, although I must say it is quite astonishing."

"Can you read my thoughts?" asked Gemma, getting carried away.

"No, I'm not a mind-reader, but I do have certain...powers, which enable me to tell a lie from the truth, and to know if someone is good or evil."

"So you can *really* foretell the future?" she asked eagerly, wondering if he knew what was in store for Atlantis.

"Yes, I am blessed with the ability to see into the future. But this mystical knowledge does not necessarily mean that I am able to change things, however much I may want to," he added honestly. "At night, I read the constellations in the heavens. The moon and the stars are an excellent source of prediction."

Rising slowly from his chair, he stood beside the crystal pool. Gemma looked at his hands. They were gnarled and wrinkled with age, and reminded her affectionately of her grandpa.

"I also see the future here," continued Pico, pointing. "This is the Pool of Destiny. It holds the truths of the universe in its depths." Shaking his head sorrowfully, he added, "But I'm afraid its power is fading fast." He gazed nostalgically at his own reflection in the water. "Without the Gem Star, its energy can never be restored."

"The Gem Star?"

"The most precious crystal in Atlantis," nodded Pico.

Gemma was intrigued. "Where is it?"

"It is kept in a secret place on the summit of a volcano. It is hidden there to prevent it from falling into the wrong hands and to protect its powers from being abused."

"If you know where it is, why don't you go and get it so that you can save the Pool of Destiny?" said Gemma matter-of-factly.

"I am too old to go on the quest – older than anyone else in Atlantis. The people refer to me as the immortal one." He smiled at the thought of his popular title. "I need someone young and trustworthy to climb up Fire Mountain and bring the crystal safely back to the city for me."

"Surely there are lots of young Atlanteans who would do that for you," she reasoned.

"Ah yes, but it is not as simple as that," he said sadly. "You see, only a true believer may touch the crystal, and people no longer believe in its existence. No one living in the city has ever seen the Gem Star, except me when I was very young. People think that it is just a myth."

Gemma smiled reassuringly. "I believe you – I believe in all kinds of magic." She touched her necklace as she said so.

"No matter where we are in history, the world will always be filled with sceptics," said Pico. "I have already seen the fate of Atlantis reflected in the Pool of Destiny. It will be destroyed by a volcanic catastrophe and will disappear into the sea for ever." His eyes brimmed with tears as he remembered the vision. "I have warned the people of their destiny. I wanted them to leave this place and live elsewhere, to travel the world and make new homes for themselves. That way, the spirit of Atlantis will live on and the knowledge we have learned can be shared with other civilisations and future generations."

"How did they react to your prediction? Did they believe you?" asked Gemma.

"No. In truth, I do not think they wanted to believe me. Even the six wise leaders of the city were not convinced," Pico explained. "And when I tried to show them what I had seen, the image was not strong enough for them to see it clearly."

"That's really sad," sympathised Gemma.

He gazed sorrowfully into the water. "The power is fading. It must have the energy of the Gem Star to restore it."

"But there must be *someone* you could send to collect the crystal," she insisted.

"I have a granddaughter, Flores. She is a lovely girl – about your age – but although she wants very much to believe in the existence of the crystal, in her heart of hearts she is not convinced. Any shadow of doubt prevents her from being able to proceed with the quest – it is not enough that she wants to help me."

"Have you no other relatives or friends?"

"Sadly, my most trusted friends have long since departed this world. They understood the old ways and how Atlantis used to be. My only other distant relation is a boy – Corvo." Pico sighed, as if the thought of the boy irked him in some way. He went on to explain. "I had hoped that Corvo would follow in my footsteps, but his heart is cruel and cold. I can never trust him or his friend, Velas. If they find the Gem Star, I fear they would take great pleasure in destroying it."

Gemma wrinkled her nose at the thought of them. "They sound *horrible*."

He nodded solemnly. "Unfortunate boys."

Then a thought occurred to her. "Must it be someone from Atlantis who finds the crystal?"

Pico looked at her, questioningly. "Are you suggesting that you might journey to Fire Mountain?"

Gemma looked hopeful. "Well, I'd be more than willing to go. I'd like to help you – if I can."

Shaking his head, Pico said, "No. It is a difficult task – too difficult."

"Well, surely we won't know just how difficult unless we try..." Gemma cajoled.

He looked pensive. "If you belong to the future as you say you do, you must know the history of the past."

"Yes," she replied, anticipating that he was going to ask her a very awkward question.

"Was my vision of disaster correct?" he asked solemnly. "Does Atlantis descend into the depths of the sea for ever?"

Words deserted her; she made an effort to shrug the subject away.

"Please tell me," he urged her.

Reluctantly, she admitted that Atlantis did disappear, adding gently, "But there are lots of myths surrounding what really happened." And then, more optimistically, "No one knows for certain."

"Although my sight is fading, I can see that restoring the Gem Star to its rightful place is now more important than ever," said Pico decisively. "If the city's leaders witness the vision for themselves, I am sure they will encourage the people to live somewhere safe."

"Where is the crystal's rightful place?" queried Gemma.

He spread his arms wide. "Here, in this cavern, deep in the sunken heart of the city."

She gazed around in amazement. "Are you saying that we're underground?"

"We are underwater!" he corrected. "Far, far below the surface of the Twin Lakes. This is a secret and sacred place. Only the wise leaders are allowed to visit this place; others must seek special permission to enter."

Gemma bit her lower lip. "Oh," she said, realising she wasn't supposed to be in the cavern at all.

He smiled warmly. "But you are very welcome. Come, let me show you where the gem originally belonged."

She followed him over to a star-shaped impression on the cavern wall. His long, flowing, turquoise robes made him appear as if he were gliding across the ground.

"This is where the gem used to be," he said, feeling the impression with his gnarled fingers. "Every hundred years, it was taken down and placed in the Pool of Destiny, to refresh the water's energy source. This century is almost at a close, and the pool's power is waning."

Gemma traced the five-pointed outline with her fingers, guessing that the gem would easily fit into her palm. "Doesn't this impression convince the leaders that the Gem Star exists?"

Pico sighed heavily. "They dismiss it as part of the myth, saying it's just a natural formation within the crystal wall."

"But it's a perfect star!" she reasoned.

He agreed. "The crystal itself is flawless. The five points relate to the natural elements of Atlantis – water, earth, fire, wood and crystal. Each part of the city is represented by an element – the lakes, the land, the volcanoes, the forests, and the crystal gems which we use as a source of energy. Together they reflect the natural balance of life."

Gemma was determined now. "I'd be willing to go on the quest for the Gem Star. Please let me do this for you."

Pico mulled her request over in his mind. This was an important decision, and one which needed careful consideration.

"The journey to Fire Mountain could be dangerous," he warned. "You would have to navigate your way through a maze of underground caverns to reach the Twin Lakes – and that would only be the beginning." Gemma remembered the two lakes near where she was staying – perhaps there was a connection.

"I've seen the lakes!" she piped up enthusiastically. "I think they still exist in the future, on an island in a place known as the Azores."

He smiled quietly, pleased to know that

perhaps part of Atlantis had survived through the ages.

"I would be very grateful for your help, Gemma, but it would not be a wise decision for me to send you on such a hazardous journey."

Undeterred, she turned and walked towards the crystal pool. "You said the Pool of Destiny holds the truths of the universe. I know its power is weak, but can't you do something to increase its energy, even for a moment, just to see whether I should go? We won't be using up lots of energy for this purpose – we only need to ask a tiny question, not look a long way into the future. Surely the remaining power will let us do that."

Pico brightened, as if she had sparked off a possibility. He pointed sagely to the tiny gemstones overflowing from the seashells.

"Choose an aquamarine, a peridot and a citrine, and drop them into the water," he instructed. "There is a chance their natural vibrations will create a brief burst of energy, and we may catch a glimpse of the answer we are searching for."

With his help, she selected the gems. Each stone was identified by its colour and clarity – the light blue of the aquamarine, the pale green peridot, and the yellow citrine. Each one sparkled prettily in her palm.

Pico stood beside her now. "Cast them into the Pool of Destiny."

A ripple of excitement flooded through her. "What will happen?"

"If the water becomes dark, then you should not go to Fire Mountain. If it turns bright blue and reflects an image of the volcano, this bodes well for you – and I will let you go."

"And will I be able to retrieve the Gem Star successfully?"

"Only time will tell that," said Pico.

Brimming with anticipation, Gemma dropped the gems into the pool's glistening depths. Within seconds, the water turned a luminous blue and the centre glowed with a strange aura, creating a faint reflection of the volcanic mountain. The image lasted only for a moment, then disappeared.

Gemma was amazed – and excited.

"Wow! Does this mean that I can go on the quest?"

She looked at Pico who was smiling warmly at her.

"Tell me the way to Fire Mountain," she enthused. "I'll do my best to bring the crystal back here safely to you."

Rummaging through the folds of his robe, Pico presented her with a parchment map and gave her instructions.

Gemma studied the map carefully. It highlighted a route through the underground maze – a special route, which Pico said would test her belief in the Gem Star. It was the one true path to the crystal.

3. The Tunnel of Fear

Gemma stood nervously at the entrance of the maze, gazing into its elaborate depths. She was completely in awe of the sight before her. A glistening labyrinth of caverns stretched away like a vast crystal honeycomb.

Pico had directed her here. Before leaving her on her own, he had wished her luck. I'm going to need it! she thought to herself, especially as her first task was to get through the Tunnel of Fear.

She had navigated her way through all sorts of mazes when she'd visited theme parks with her family, but this was something else entirely – a mystical dimension, deep below the surface of the Twin Lakes. Well, Pico was depending on her.

Taking a deep breath, she unfolded the parchment map and studied the brightly-coloured markings which highlighted the route. She read the messages beside them.

'Tunnel of Fear' was written in ghostly green, with the warning words,

Beware the terrifying darkness
And eerie voices.
Within the green shadows
Await two choices.

This did little to boost Gemma's confidence, and she began to have niggling second thoughts about the whole idea. She should have read the map properly before setting off, then she could have asked Pico's advice – but now she'd have to work it out for herself.

Tucking the map away in the pocket of her jeans, she gave herself a good talking to. "All you have to do is follow the directions and you won't get lost."

Stepping forth into the crystal honeycomb, she headed, as the map instructed, for the third opening on the right.

"One...two...three," she counted.

This led her into a circular passageway. Its walls were covered with amethysts which glittered with a purple radiance. According to the map, Gemma had to walk through here to reach the Tunnel of Fear.

At first, cool air wafted gently through the passage, but the further in she ventured, the stronger the breeze became, until it was blowing her hair back from her face with gale-force gusts.

Leaning forward into the wind, Gemma tried to make headway, but the wind was so powerful that she could hardly breathe. Gasping, she struggled onwards, determined to complete the last few blustery steps.

With a sigh of relief, she finally reached the exit. As she did so, the strange wind ceased, as if someone somewhere had suddenly turned it off.

Now she was standing before the Tunnel of Fear. She gulped. Just looking at the ghostly-green mist that floated from the tunnel's arched entrance was enough to make her hair stand on end. Gemma's hands began to sweat nervously, as deep within the tunnel she could hear hideous sounds echoing. Icy shivers tingled down her spine.

"Time to check the map again," she murmured, pulling it from her pocket and studying it anxiously. She hoped to find an alternative route, but she was out of luck. This was the only way. She read the message.

*Head for the darkness to seal your fate.
Once there, do not hesitate.
The Tunnel of Fear will tell you what to do.
Listen to your heart to know what is true.*

Gemma sighed with frustration. "I don't like the sound of all this mumbo-jumbo. Why can't the message be in simple plain English?"

Like it or not, this was where she had to go. Forcing herself to be brave, she approached the tunnel, watching as the green mist swirled and enveloped her. Peering through it Gemma could see a rusty track which faded into the distance. On it stood an empty carriage – presumably waiting for her. Cautiously, she climbed in and sat down.

The carriage began to move slowly, trundling her into the tunnel, where it gradually began to pick up speed.

Clutching on to the edge of her seat, the message on the map repeated itself in her mind:

The Tunnel of Fear will tell you what to do. Listen to your heart to know what is true.

All Gemma could see before her was swirling mist spiralling into unearthly shapes, then fading into nothing as she whizzed past. Strange sounds echoed around her, and an eerie voice whispered her name, "Gemma!"

"Gemma!" The voice whispered again.

"Who...who are you?" she stammered. The voice laughed back at her.

Was it her imagination, or did she sense

its delight in scaring her?

"I'm not frightened of you," she called out, trying to sound brave.

"Don't tell lies, Gemma," it warned her.

"You don't scare me," she bluffed, shouting with as much defiance as she could muster.

There was an eerie silence. She waited with baited breath. Had this done the trick?

Suddenly, the carriage came to an abrupt halt, and the mist deepened to a greenish-black, spiralling around her. She trembled – what was happening now?

"Are you scared of the dark?" the voice whispered.

Don't give in now, she told herself firmly. If it senses your fear, you may never escape.

"No, of course I'm not," she lied.

There was silence again.

"Two openings lead from the Tunnel of Fear," said the voice. "One way leads to danger, the other to safety. Which way will you choose?"

Two doorways emerged up ahead. Luminous green mist filtered from the stone door on the left. Gemma stared at the door on the right, but could see nothing but a fathomless black void.

"Which one will you choose?" the weird voice repeated.

Gemma remembered the advice on the map, and tried to follow her heart.

"I choose the door of darkness," she said, crossing her fingers and hoping that her instincts were right.

"A wise choice, Gemma," the voice murmured, then faded away.

Climbing out of the carriage, she walked over to the black void, putting one hand in to see what was there, but she could feel nothing.

"Okay, here goes."

Stepping inside, she was surprised when the darkness vanished instantly. With a sigh of relief, she realised that now she was safe in another part of the crystal maze.

"Where to now?" she whispered to herself, pulling the map from her pocket. At that moment, she had the distinct feeling that someone was watching her. She glanced around uneasily, but couldn't see anyone.

Shrugging, she turned to read the next part of the journey.

*Follow the steps of amber
Which lead to the Serpent's Slide.
Far below lurks friend or foe,
Let destiny decide.*

Convinced that she was heading in the right direction, she carried on reading the map as she wound her way through the maze. The route twisted and turned, and there were a few dead ends, but she made good progress.

Still, she couldn't shake off the overwhelming, creeping feeling that she was being followed, but every time she looked back there was no one there.

Sighing to herself, she paused for a moment and studied the map, tracing the best route with her finger and memorising it. Just then, a dark shadow fell over her and Gemma looked up in fright.

Two shadows loomed ominously on the wall ahead of her. Her blood turned cold, freezing her to the spot.

"Give me the map," whispered a voice from behind her.

A hand touched her shoulder, and she jumped at the feel of it.

Spinning around, she came face to face with two boys, both of whom she judged to be around fourteen years old.

Perhaps this was Corvo and Velas – Pico had warned her that they sometimes came here without his permission.

"I saw you talking to Pico," one of them said, confirming Gemma's suspicions.

Looking at him, Gemma could see a resemblance. His eyes too were pale blue but, unlike Pico, his hair was as dark as a raven.

"You must be Corvo," she said.

He raised his eyebrows sceptically. "Pico told you about me?"

"Yes, he mentioned you and Velas."

Corvo looked her up and down. "Where are you from?" he asked suspiciously. Gemma didn't comment.

"Who are you?" said Velas, narrowing his grey eyes as he stared at her.

"I have to be going," she insisted, trying to sidestep them and their questions.

Corvo put a restraining arm across her path. "You're going nowhere until you tell us what you're up to."

The menace in his voice was clear, but Gemma was determined not to give in to their bullying.

"I'm Gemma James, and what I'm doing is none of your business!"

"Take the map from her," Velas snapped impatiently at his friend.

Corvo did so, snatching it forcefully from her hand.

"How dare you!" cried Gemma angrily, surprised at how confident she sounded. She snatched it back and ran off as fast as she could. Don't look back, she said to herself. Just keep running.

The boys called out and ran after her, but Gemma was faster, darting through the crystal maze. As she sprinted around a corner, she could see an orangey-yellow stairway spiralling upwards ahead of her. The steps of amber!

Bounding up the stairs, she reached the

top and was confronted by the Serpent's Slide – a slithery, high-speed chute that coiled downwards to a deep blue lagoon.

"Quickly!" shouted Corvo. "Grab her before she goes down the slide."

The boys rushed towards her, their faces red with anger, determined that she would not get away.

Gemma glanced at the slide. It's now or never, she told herself, realising that the snake-like chute was her only means of escape. She jammed the map into her pocket and began her descent feet first down the slippery slope. Faster and faster she flew, spiralling downwards at a terrific speed towards the water far below.

Reaching the bottom, she plunged into the lagoon, the water ice cold against her skin. Opening her eyes, she began to swim upwards, heading for the light of the surface. She came up gasping and spluttering for air.

Corvo and Velas hadn't followed her. She could see them watching from the top of the Serpent's Slide. What was wrong? Were they scared, or were they planning to go by another route?

Gemma's moment of triumph came to an abrupt end. She screamed in horror, as a huge tentacle lashed out at her, missing her by a fraction. Turning, she saw giant bubbles gurgling in the middle of the lagoon, a sure sign that something – presumably the creature to which the tentacle belonged – was about to surface at any second.

From the depths of the water, the head of an enormous sea monster surged upwards, searching for its prey. Dark, greenish-brown scales covered its repulsive body. To Gemma, it looked like a cross between a giant octopus and a dragon. Instinctively she screamed, swimming furiously towards the edge of the lagoon, as the monster's tentacles reached out to catch her. Terror made her muscles tense; she slowed down. Everything felt as if it was happening in slow motion.

Safety was now within reach, but Gemma panicked – could she grab the edge in time? The monster was gaining on her; she could feel its tentacles against her toes, and she struggled to get away.

From their vantage point, Corvo and Velas laughed, their amusement echoing around the cavern. The sound of their laughter made Gemma look up, and as she did so she noticed what she hoped might be a quicker way to escape.

Large, pointed crystals and thick spirals of sea coral hung down like stalactites from the roof of the cavern encasing the lagoon. If she could just reach one she might be able to escape. She struggled to grab hold of the coral and at last her wet hand made contact. Clinging to it gratefully, she climbed up the spiral to safety before the creature entwined her. Its tentacles made a final, desperate attempt to ensnare her, but she scrambled out of its deadly reach.

With a terrific splash, the monster disappeared into the depths of the lagoon. Exhausted, Gemma wanted to rest, but she knew that she had to keep going. Dripping wet, but safely out of harm's way, she pulled the map from her pocket and laid it flat on the ground, worried that the ink might run because the parchment was soaking.

Recognising roughly where she was, Gemma realised that there was only one more obstacle to overcome. She headed thankfully into the maze once more, shaking her wet hair as she went. Instinct and the bright glow of daylight was her compass as she tried to find the Walls of Doom marked on her map.

The path led out of the maze, and as she approached the towering stone exit she caught a tempting glimpse of the shimmering lakes in the distance.

She had to pass through one more corridor, but as she looked ahead, she could see that the walls were moving! The entire sides of the maze crashed in and out in an irregular pattern, threatening to crush anyone who dared to walk between them.

"The symbols of the night will lead your way," she read aloud, looking at the details on the map. "Don't be fooled by what they say."

Gemma could see a strange assortment of symbols carved on the paved floor

45

between the walls. It was easy to identify a star, a sun, a bat, a tree, an owl, a flower and a moon. Three other symbols lay ahead of her, but they were too far away for her to see clearly.

Surely the star was the first symbol of the night. Gauging her timing, Gemma ran forward and stepped on to the star stone. The Walls of Doom didn't move. Next, she stepped over the sun and on to the bat. The Walls of Doom still did not move – she had made the right choice again. So far, so good.

Nervously, she stepped across the tree and on to the owl, then over the flower to the moon. She paused to study the last three symbols: a man, a sundial and a candle. The message on the map flashed through her mind as she puzzled over these last three steps.

The symbols of the night
Will lead your way.
Don't be fooled by what they say.

Gemma reasoned with herself. By nature,

human beings are active during daylight hours and they sleep at night, so she would have to avoid stepping on the stone engraved with a man. As for the sundial, it told the time from the shadows cast by the sun, so presumably this stone must be avoided too. Finally, she looked at the candle. Surely *this* was a symbol of the night. She would have to leap over the man and the sundial to land safely on the candle stone.

It was quite a jump. Steadying herself on the edge of the moon stone, Gemma coiled back ready to spring across.

"Ready, steady...Oh no! Of course..." she exclaimed, realising her mistake. The symbols of the sundial and the candle had fooled her. The candle had no flame, and the sundial had no shadow. An unlit candle indicated day, and a shadowless sundial would only be found at night. She'd got the symbols the wrong way round! Realising too late, she landed on the candle stone. As she did so, a low rumbling sound like thunder shook the Walls of Doom.

Gemma could see that the walls were

closing in on her. With no time to spare, she made a frantic dash between the walls, just managing to slip through safely.

Behind her, the walls slammed shut, and the cavern echoed with the rumbling vibrations. Sighing with relief, Gemma realised that she had only just escaped in time.

4. Flores and the Sapphire Lake

The sky above the shimmering Twin Lakes was a cloudless, turquoise blue.

Gemma stood outside the maze, tilting her face towards the welcoming sunshine. She breathed in the warm, fresh air, fragrant with exotic, sweet-scented flowers. Now I can dry off, she thought delightedly to herself.

Just ahead, fringed by long grass and leafy plants, lay the Emerald Lake. Adjoining it, the Sapphire Lake was as smooth as glass.

Gemma sighed to herself, wishing that the twentieth century could see the wonders of Atlantis, too. It easily surpassed all the myths and legends that she'd read about in her history books. "I feel like a fairy-tale princess in a watercolour painting," she whispered dreamily to herself.

Far off on the horizon, she could see her next destination – the Azure Forest. In order to reach it she must sail across the Sapphire Lake. Pico had told her where she would be able to find a canoe, but her main concern was to cross the lake without being noticed by any Atlantean people. Pico had warned her that they would not accept her as readily as he, so she had been instructed to keep out of sight.

In the distance, on the opposite side of the lakes, Gemma noticed some people, but they were too far away to see her. As she approached the place where Pico had said that she would find the canoe, Gemma saw a young girl playing; she appeared to be alone.

Gemma's heart sank – yet another obstacle to overcome!

Hiding in the long grass, she decided to

wait until the girl had gone. She had no choice now but to watch her play at the edge of the lake.

The girl had long, dark hair which fell to her waist, and she wore a purple dress. She had sandals on her feet, and Gemma noticed that she was wearing what looked like an amethyst bracelet, too.

Moments later, Gemma saw Corvo and Velas approach the girl, still looking as hostile as they had when she'd met them the first time.

She crouched down out of sight to listen to their conversation.

"Do your parents know you're here?" Corvo said to the girl spitefully.

"No, but I'm not doing anything wrong," she replied nervously.

"Perhaps I should tell them what you've been up to," threatened Corvo nastily.

"Don't do that, Corvo," she pleaded.

He turned to Velas. "What do you think? Should we tell them we saw their precious Flores at the lakes?"

Flores! Gemma mouthed silently. The girl was Pico's granddaughter.

Although she must have been around the same age as Gemma, she was smaller in height and build. The boys towered over her, taking great pleasure in bullying her.

"If you tell us about Gemma, we'll keep quiet about you being here," snapped Velas.

Flores looked scared and puzzled. "Who's Gemma?"

Corvo sounded angry and impatient. "She's the strange-looking girl who we met in the crystal maze." He glanced around. "Have you seen her? She must have come

51

this way."

"That's if the monster of the lagoon didn't get her first," laughed Velas gleefully. "Maybe we should feed Flores to the creature, too," he added.

The girl's violet eyes widened with fright and glistened with tears. "I don't know what you're talking about."

Corvo prodded her shoulder with a jabbing finger. "Don't lie to me. We saw Pico give her a map. The two of them are up to something, and I want to know what it is."

"I'm not lying," she said shakily.

Gemma was sorely tempted to rush to the girl's defence, but she couldn't risk it. Powerless, she felt the anger well up inside her, but knew she must stay reluctantly hidden in the grass.

"Where is Gemma?" Corvo demanded again.

"I've no idea," said Flores, pleading her innocence.

Corvo's eyes narrowed. "Pico confides in you, we know he does. Don't pretend to be innocent – you must know where she is."

"But I don't!" protested Flores. "And

Grandfather has never mentioned her."

"You expect us to believe that?" argued Velas.

"Why not? It's true!" she said tearfully.

Corvo grabbed her sharply by the arm, pulled her close and shouted into her face. "I'm going to ask you one last time, and if you don't tell me who Gemma is, I swear I'll throw you in the lake."

"I don't *know!*" she cried, struggling unsuccessfully to break free.

"Come on, Corvo, we're wasting our breath," Velas muttered angrily. Corvo tossed his head.

To her dismay, Gemma watched as the two boys grabbed Flores and pushed her into the lake. Then they ran off laughing. Quickly, Gemma dashed to the girl's rescue. Flores obviously wasn't a very good swimmer – she was splashing and struggling to keep her head above the deep blue water.

Gemma knelt down at the edge of the lake and reached out to her. "Give me your hand!" she shouted.

The girl was panicking in her efforts to get back to shore.

Gemma shouted encouragement. "Come on, Flores, you can do it!"

The girl grabbed hold of Gemma's outstretched hand, and felt herself being pulled safely on to dry land.

Soaking wet, she lay on the grass, gasping and spluttering for breath.

Gemma bent down beside her. "Are you all right?"

Flores coughed for a moment, then managed to sit up. "Yes, I think so – thank you." She pushed her long, wet hair back from her face, and stared at her rescuer in astonishment. "Who are you?"

"I'm Gemma – Gemma James. I saw what Corvo and Velas did to you. They're really mean."

Flores tried to piece together what was going on. "Do you know my grandfather? Corvo said he gave you a map. Is that true?"

"Yes it is, but it's a secret – you mustn't tell anyone you saw me," Gemma explained.

"A secret?" Flores looked excited.

Gemma nodded. "Promise you'll keep quiet?"

"I promise," Flores said. "But tell me

this – has the map got anything to do with finding the Gem Star?"

Gemma was surprised at Flores' quick thinking.

"That's the secret, isn't it?" concluded Flores. "I've seen the map. Grandfather showed it to me."

"Yes, but you mustn't tell. Pico is depending on me to bring the crystal back to the city."

A shadow fell upon the girl's lovely face. "I wanted to help Grandfather, but I didn't really believe in the Gem Star. He said I couldn't go on the quest if there was any doubt whatsoever in my mind."

"Well, he doesn't blame you, so don't feel bad about it," Gemma reassured her.

"You still haven't explained who you are, and what you're doing here."

Gemma spoke cautiously. "If I tell you, I need you to promise never to reveal my secrets without Pico's permission."

"Of course. I wouldn't do anything against his wishes."

Gemma took a deep breath and started to explain. "Do you believe in magic?"

"Oh yes, one day I want to be a seer just like Grandfather."

Good, thought Gemma – hopefully Flores will understand. "This is a magic necklace," she confided, touching her sparkling beads. "I don't have time to explain everything, but the power of this necklace brought me here to Atlantis."

Flores' eyes opened wide with wonder.

Gemma continued. "My magic jewellery enables me to travel back in time to faraway lands."

"What land do you come from?" gasped Flores.

"I live in the future, thousands of years from now."

Flores was speechless.

"I know it's difficult to take in, but honestly, it's true."

"No wonder you look so strange," Flores remarked, smiling. "Did you come here to help my grandfather? Did he summon you to Atlantis?"

"No, he didn't. I just wanted to visit this world, but after I met Pico I offered to help him."

"Do you have magic powers, too?"

"No – my jewellery is magical, but I don't have any special powers."

Flores seemed puzzled. "So why did Pico choose you to go on the quest for the Gem Star?"

"Because..." Gemma hesitated, her voice trailing off to a whisper.

The girl's eyes misted over, suddenly realising the answer. "Because you're from the future and you know what happens to Atlantis. Pico's vision of the city sinking into the sea is true, isn't it?"

Gemma nodded sadly. "Some legends say the city was destroyed by a volcanic catastrophe, but there are so many myths, no one knows for sure what really happened. In fact, most people in the modern world don't believe Atlantis ever existed – they think it's *all* just a myth."

Flores looked at her imploringly. "Is there anything we can do to save the city?"

"No matter what we do, Atlantis will disappear, but if I can find the Gem Star it will confirm Pico's vision. It will serve as a warning, giving the people time to leave the city for somewhere safe. That's why it's so important for the crystal to be returned to its rightful place."

"Let me help you, Gemma."

"It could be dangerous."

Flores brushed her warning aside. "I've seen the map and I understand the dangers, but I know this area very well and I'd like to help you as much as I can."

Gemma considered her suggestion. It would be a real advantage having someone to help her, especially someone who knew the hazards which they might be up against. "Okay, we'll go together," she said, making up her mind. Unfolding the map, she laid it on the grass so that they could both study it carefully.

As they crouched down together, Gemma read the next message.

Sail across the Sapphire Lake.
Be alert, stay awake.
The Azure Forest you will see,
And this may be your destiny.
Enter the forest if you dare.
Superstitions await you there.

She turned to Flores. "Any idea what it means?"

Flores looked thoughtful. "Yes, I think so. Although the lake appears to be smooth and calm, it's full of hidden whirlpools. We'll have to be wary of them. And a vapour rises from the water which makes you feel sleepy, so it's essential that we stay awake."

"What about the forest?"

"Few people ever venture there because they're frightened of the blue mist and strange superstitions."

"I'm not superstitious," said Gemma. "Are you afraid?"

"A little, but Grandfather has told me all about the mystic forest. If we're careful, I'm sure we'll be fine."

Gemma smiled at Flores – things were looking up now that she had someone to confide in.

The girls found the canoe where Pico had said it would be and they climbed in, paddling smoothly out across the Sapphire Lake.

Unbeknown to them, Corvo and Velas

had witnessed their meeting and were watching and waiting to follow in their wake.

5. The Flames of Wrath

A heady perfume wafted from the tranquil waters of the Sapphire Lake, lulling Gemma and Flores into a dreamy sleep.

"It's so relaxing here," Gemma murmured drowsily, feeling her eyelids grow heavy, as if she were slowly being hypnotised.

"We must stay awake," Flores reminded her sleepily.

Gemma shook herself. She stopped paddling for a moment, dipped her hands into the lake and splashed the cool water on to her face to wake herself up. Flores did the same, blinking as the water splashed into her eyes.

Distracted, they had allowed the canoe to drift for a few moments.

"Look out!" cried Gemma, seeing the ripples of a whirlpool just ahead of them.

Flores leaped into action. "Quickly, paddle to the left of it!"

Together they steered the canoe out of danger, only to find another whirlpool eddying in their path. This time they veered to the right, to avoid being sucked into its swirling depths.

Paddling with all their might, the two girls worked their way across the lake, and landed on the deserted, pebbled shore of the Azure Forest.

"What a weird-looking place," remarked Gemma, as they dragged the canoe ashore and sat down at the edge of the dark woodland. The trees were a deep silvery-blue colour, shrouded in an azure mist. "We seem to be the only people here," she added, trying to dismiss a growing sense of unease which was making her shiver.

"Oh," explained Flores, "that's because the superstitions keep people away."

"What are the superstitions?" said Gemma, although she wasn't sure she really wanted to hear them.

Flores stared into the depths of the forest. "The blue mist is said to be the evil souls of dead people."

Gemma laughed nervously, then shuddered to herself – I knew I shouldn't have asked!

Flores continued. "We'll have to watch out for the Jealous Trees – their branches are tipped with a dark green poison. Then there's the superstition about the Flames of Wrath, where the ground bursts into fire when you walk on it."

"Jealous Trees! Flames of Wrath! You must be joking," Gemma said, but Flores was deadly serious. She looked at Gemma solemnly. "If you don't believe me, we might as well give up right now, because we won't get any further..."

"I'm sorry," said Gemma, hastily correcting herself. Then she remembered something. "Wait a minute," she said. Digging deep into her jeans pocket, she pulled out a clear, bright yellow citrine. The gem looked like a little piece of sunshine in this creepy place. "Pico gave me this. He said it would help protect me in the Azure Forest."

Flores looked pleased. "It's a mystic citrine – very powerful for fending off evil."

"Does it really work?" asked Gemma dubiously.

"Oh yes, but we'll still have to be careful. The forest is a dangerous place."

Gemma looked at the map. "Right, let's see what we have to do next." She read the instructions which were written in bold blue lettering.

*The mist may trap you here forever,
Unless you reach the silver river.*

"The river is beyond those trees," said Flores, pointing to their mysterious shadows.

"Come on – let's go!" said Gemma impatiently, clutching tightly to the citrine; she had no intention of sitting there any longer.

As soon as they entered the forest, the girls were engulfed by an eerie blue darkness. Staying close together, they made tentative progress.

"It's so quiet," whispered Gemma. "You could hear a pin drop around here!"

"I've never been this far into the forest," Flores confided quietly. "My father brought me here last year, but we didn't go any further than the first line of trees."

Now she tells me! thought Gemma. She peered into the mist. "I can't see the river, can you?"

"No, and I can't hear it, either."

"In fact, I can't hear anything at all," remarked Gemma. Just then, a loud, ear-piercing shriek rang out through the silence. Gemma stopped dead in her tracks.

"What on *earth* was that?"

"I don't know, but it didn't sound like an animal or a bird."

"And it didn't sound quite human, either," Gemma whispered anxiously.

Another shriek shattered the silence, even louder than the first.

Gemma jumped. "I don't like the sound of that at all."

"Neither do I."

"Does the citrine really have the power to protect us?" asked Gemma hopefully.

"Yes," said Flores. "Hold it up in front of us and it should act like a protective shield."

Gemma held the gem at arm's length, hoping what Flores believed was actually true.

"Stay close to me," she whispered, as they carried on.

The mist grew thicker, forming human-like shadows which howled and shrieked in torment. As the girls walked, the shapes towered over them, then disappeared into nothing.

"This is awful!" cried Flores.

"Just keep walking – try not to think about it!" Gemma said firmly.

Just then, she caught a glimpse of silver gleaming through the trees. "We're nearly there! Look, there's the river. We've got to keep going now."

The shadows grew larger and more menacing, seeming to block the girls' way as they floated in front of them. Their howling chilled Gemma and Flores to the bone. Gemma's hands shook. She almost dropped the gem as she thrust it at the shadows in a desperate attempt to make them disappear.

For a moment nothing happened, then the citrine began to shine with a bright yellow glow. A beam of light shot out and cut through the shadows and they screamed in rage, disappearing as they were destroyed by the gem's power.

The girls clung to each other, watching fearfully as the shadowy figures began to shrink and shrivel into heaps of dark blue dust.

Gemma grimaced. "Ugh! That was horrible. Thank goodness we're safe."

"Think again," a threatening voice echoed from behind them.

Spinning around, the girls were

confronted by the menacing figures of Corvo and Velas.

"Give me the map," Corvo demanded.

"Not on your life!" Gemma retaliated. "Run, Flores, run!" Grabbing hold of her friend's hand, she dragged her off through the trees. They raced towards the river, the boys in hot pursuit.

"Watch out for the Jealous Trees," Flores warned her.

Quickly and nimbly, they scampered through the gaps between the trunks. The citrine felt as warm as sunshine in Gemma's hand, and she sensed that it was helping to protect them against the boys. Suddenly, there was a cry from behind and Gemma turned to see Corvo entangled in the branches. The deadly points had just missed piercing his skin. Velas was frustratedly pulling him free. Delighted, Gemma and Flores hurried on, making headway.

Safely past the trees, the girls raced towards the river, pausing for a moment when they reached its glittering banks.

Gemma gazed in amazement. "It

doesn't look real!" she gasped. "The water looks just like liquid silver."

"What are we going to do?" asked Flores anxiously. The boys were catching up.

"Well, there's no time to read the map now," said Gemma. "We'll simply have to take a chance and cross the river."

Flores nodded. Anything was better than facing Corvo and Velas.

Gemma stepped knee-deep into the metallic-looking water. "It seems to be quite shallow. I think we should be able to wade across."

Together they tentatively began to make their way to the other side. At its deepest point, the river came up to their waists.

"You won't get away from us!" Corvo shouted at them.

Gemma glanced over her shoulder and saw that the boys were already wading after them.

"They'll catch us!" cried Flores.

"Not if we keep going. Come on – we're almost there now," Gemma reassured her.

Flores did her best to trail through the silvery water as fast as she could, and soon they both arrived at the other side.

"Where do we go now?"

Gemma took out the map and studied the next part of the route. "Crossing the river was the right choice, I think – but now I'm afraid we have to head for the Flames of Wrath."

There was a cry as Velas stumbled and fell headfirst into the silver river. Corvo, who was way ahead of him, was forced to turn back to help him. Gemma read on.

Tread warily on the Flames of Wrath.
The hardest way is the chosen path.

"What do you suppose it means?" Flores wondered.

Gemma looked at the ground. Some parts of it appeared to be dry and cracked, and gnarled with tree roots, while others seemed soft and springy, with patches of grass. "I think it means we should walk on the hard ground if we want to avoid the flames," she reasoned.

Flores glanced back at the boys. Corvo had pulled Velas to his feet. "Here they come," she warned.

"Right," said Gemma. "I'll go first, you follow in my footsteps."

Flores nodded in agreement.

Gemma took a tentative step forward, concentrating on avoiding the soft earth. Flores followed her every step, and soon they were halfway across the dangerous ground. Step by step they continued, stopping only when the threatening voices of the boys called out to taunt them.

"You'll never get away, Flores," shouted Corvo. "One way or another, you're going to perish in that forest."

Startled, Flores lost her balance, almost stumbling on to a soft piece of earth which would have instantly burst into flames.

"Don't let them scare you," Gemma reassured her. "As long as we keep to the hard ground we'll be perfectly all right."

"You're right, Gemma, we can do this."

Behind them, Corvo and Velas were deciding on the best way to follow the girls through the Flames of Wrath. They had heard how the ground could burst into flames but, without the map, they didn't know where they could safely step.

Corvo, who had been watching the girls, tried to remember the path they had taken.

"Follow me," he said to Velas confidently.

The first few steps were fine, but then Corvo made the mistake of treading on a piece of soft earth. The ground erupted into blazing flames around his feet, and he leaped backwards to avoid being badly burned.

"Don't look back at them," said Gemma, "concentrate on where we're walking."

"How much further do we have to go before we find our way out of this forest?" said Flores, who was feeling really tired.

"It's not far now."

Seconds later, the ground before their feet gave way, and a gaping crevasse opened in the earth like a huge mouth ready to swallow them. Boiling water gurgled in its depths and clouds of scorching steam rose into the air.

"Jump!" shouted Gemma, leaping over the crevasse before it widened any further.

Closing her eyes, Flores jumped and landed. The earth creaked and groaned as the gaping hole stretched wider and wider, placing a hurdle between them and the boys.

Corvo raged at them. "You can't run for ever. Sooner or later we'll catch you – and then you'll both be sorry!"

Flores was shaking.

"Don't worry Flores, you're safe with me," said Gemma, putting her arm around her protectively. I'll have to talk to Pico about Corvo and Velas, she thought to herself, so that Flores is safe when I've gone.

On the opposite side of the crevasse, Corvo was still ranting and issuing threats.

Just then, Gemma felt the citrine become burning hot, almost blistering the skin on the palm of her hand.

"Ouch!" she shouted, dropping the bright yellow gem on to the ground. It glowed like a piece of fiery sun. She bent down to pick it up, but Flores stopped her.

"Don't touch it," she warned. "It will burn right through your hand."

Gemma stared in amazement as the citrine burst into life like a firework, shooting high into the air and exploding in a blaze of golden light. Hundreds of tiny burning particles floated down on to the boys, piercing their clothing like red-hot needles.

Corvo and Velas ran back through the forest towards the cool water of the silver river. In their haste, they stepped on the softened earth, causing the Flames of Wrath to erupt.

The girls watched as their two assailants disappeared into the forest.

Flores breathed a sigh of relief.

"Come on!" said Gemma. "We're not there yet..."

6. The Gem Star

Dark and dramatic, the volcanic Fire Mountain towered high above in the turquoise sky, casting a deep red shadow over the land.

The girls emerged from the edge of the Azure Forest to see the majestic mountain rising in the distance, beyond a field of rainbow-coloured flowers blowing gently in the warm summer breeze.

For as far as the eye could see, the landscape was a green and yellow patchwork of fields and flowers. An exotic fragrance lingered in the air. White stone houses dotted the faraway hillsides, and Gemma could see wild horses galloping in a field in the distance.

She stood with her back to the forest, gazing out at the scene. The dark shadows of the trees hid her from view while she checked to see if anyone was around. No, as far as she could see, she and Flores were alone.

Hearing the gurgling of a stream rippling nearby, Flores suggested that they have a drink before heading for the mountain.

Together they went over, and scooped up handfuls of the cool, refreshing water. It tasted so pure and clean.

"Where is everyone?" asked Gemma, sitting on the grassy bank. "I can't believe no one's here to make the most of this gorgeous place."

"People don't come here very often. Only those who occasionally tend the land."

"But it's so beautiful," reasoned Gemma.

"Yes – but it's dangerous too. Fire Mountain is very unpredictable – one moment everything is safe, then it changes without warning," explained Flores. "That's why the Gem Star is hidden here – the volcano protects it, so we must not make it angry."

"I know that volcanoes erupt unexpectedly, but you talk as if the mountain is alive!"

"It is."

Gemma giggled. "That's silly!"

"Don't laugh, you'll offend the mountain."

Flores' warning came a second too late. The sky grew dark and threatening.

A hush fell upon everything, as if the landscape was holding its breath, waiting in anticipation for something dangerous to happen.

Gemma stopped giggling and looked up. Flocks of birds rose from the trees and soared towards the horizon like scudding black clouds. Even the wild horses galloped away across the fields, driven by an unseen force.

"I told you that it was alive," Flores

reprimanded her. "And it sounds angry. Check the map. See what it tells us to do."

Unfolding the parchment, Gemma read the message which was written in volcanic red.

*Respect the Fire Mountain's power,
Or your soul it will devour.
If its anger you awake – watch out –
The earth will start to quake!*

"What are we going to do?" cried Flores.

"I'm not going back without the Gem Star," Gemma said firmly. She hadn't come all this way to return empty-handed. "We've come this far; there must be a safe route I can climb to reach the top of the mountain."

Flores was quick to correct her. "A safe route *we* can climb. We'll go together or not at all."

Gemma smiled at this sudden confidence from Flores, and they set off across the flowery field towards Fire Mountain.

"This is going to be really hard!" said Gemma, staring up at the craggy rock face.

"Does the map give any more advice?" Flores suggested hopefully.

Gemma checked. There was a footnote

in small red lettering.

*Climb the broken-hearted ridge,
Until you reach the invisible bridge.
Beyond the bridge is a statue of gold –
Here is a secret never to be told.*

"Look," said Flores, pointing to a strange shaped ridge further along the mountain side. The stone was a deep red colour. "Could that be the broken heart?"

Gemma stared at it keenly. "Hmm, maybe. It *has* got a big crack through the middle."

They hurried towards the huge ridge and began to climb up, using the cracks in the broken heart as hand- and footholds.

This area of the mountain seemed quite calm and peaceful, confirming the message on the map – this was their best route. The two girls paused several times to catch their breath before continuing to climb to the top of the ridge. At the top they hauled themselves on to a large, flat rock which jutted out from the mountain side.

"Phew!" gasped Gemma. "I'm shattered!"

"I never dreamed I'd ever climb Fire

Mountain," said Flores, elated at her achievement.

They sat a moment to rest and gather their strength.

"What an incredible view," sighed Gemma, gazing out over Atlantis. The Twin Lakes sparkled in the distance amidst lush greenery and buttery-yellow fields. The clean air was scented with the fragrance of the flowers, and the faraway city shone like a crystal rainbow in the sunlight.

As she sat taking in the view, Gemma felt sad to think of such beauty being destroyed. It made her even more determined to find the Gem Star and take it back to Pico. Although the fate of Atlantis was sealed, she was hopeful that most of the people could be saved, and that their civilisation would spread throughout the ancient world.

"I can't see the bridge," said Flores, screwing up her eyes in the sunshine.

"Neither can I," said Gemma. Then it dawned on her. "How can we possibly see it if it's invisible?"

Flores looked puzzled. "I don't know."

Come on – think! Gemma urged herself.

Stepping lightly to the edge of the flat rock where they sat, she tried to figure out where the bridge would be, but there were no obvious clues.

Turning to face Flores, she saw something glisten out of the corner of her eye. When she blinked and looked to see what it was, it had vanished.

Flores came over. "What is it?"

"I thought I saw something, but the moment I blinked it had gone. It was probably nothing."

"Maybe it was the bridge," said Flores excitedly.

Gemma nodded doubtfully. "Well something – whatever it was – definitely glistened."

"Where?"

"Over there." She pointed beyond the edge of the cliff face.

As they both went over to take a closer look Flores saw it shining.

"There it is. The bridge is made of crystal."

Gemma beamed. "Wow! It looks just like glass – no wonder we couldn't see it."

The bridge stretched across a wide

ravine. Long and narrow, it glistened and sparkled in the sunlight.

"Do you think it will hold our weight?" asked Flores.

"Well, Pico's map hasn't let us down so far. We'll just have to trust it, or we'll never reach the Gem Star." In a way, she was trying to convince herself as well as Flores. Gemma had never crossed a crystal bridge – how could she tell if it was safe or not?

Carefully she made the first tentative step on to the glass-like structure. "It seems solid enough."

"I'm scared," Flores admitted nervously.

"So am I, but I trust Pico, and somehow I have a feeling that this is the right way to go."

They both took a deep breath and walked across the bridge, trying not to look down.

"This has to be one of the weirdest experiences I've ever had," said Gemma. "I feel as if I'm skywalking."

"It doesn't seem so bad once you get used to it," said Flores, beginning to sound quite pleased with herself.

Soon, they made it safely across to the other side. Just above them, the top of the mountain was in sight.

"I can see the golden statue!" said Gemma, excitedly scrambling up to look at it in detail. Flores was close behind.

The statue was quite small, less than half the height of Gemma. The gold was inlaid with aquamarines, and represented the figure of a maiden wearing long flowing robes, emerging from the sea.

Flores identified the figurine. "She's the

Sea Princess. She's supposed to guard the secrets of Atlantis beneath the ocean, never revealing them to a living soul. She doesn't speak in words; her voice is the whispering sound of the sea."

"We have to find out what's inside the statue," said Gemma, feeling around with eager fingers. As she touched its gleaming contours she said, "It seems to be solid."

"Look underneath the waves," suggested Flores. "According to the legend, that's where the Sea Princess keeps her secrets."

Gemma ran her fingers over the sculptured base of the golden waves, and as she did so she activated a hidden mechanism. A dazzling light shone out from a star-shaped crystal which was mounted inside the statue. The girls' faces lit up at the sight of it – rapt in wonder at what they had found.

The Gem Star glittered more brightly than the most perfect diamond. Beams of white light danced around its exquisite five points, and as Gemma stared at it she thought it must be fashioned from the purest crystal imaginable.

Holding her breath, she reached in and

carefully lifted the magical gem out. "We've found it!" she gasped excitedly.

The star's glittering reflections sparkled in her face. Its source of mystical energy and power was almost tangible to her.

Flores smiled, and for the first time Gemma thought that she looked truly happy – but their happiness was short-lived. A crack of thunder resounded behind, making them both jump, and a strong smell of sulphur wafted through the air. The girls began to cough and choke, wondering what was happening. A low rumble echoed from the pit of Fire Mountain and it began to tremble violently, threatening to erupt at any moment.

Gemma tucked the Gem Star hastily into the pocket of her jeans. "Quickly, head for the bridge..." she shouted. "We have to get out of here before the volcano erupts."

They turned and fled towards the invisible bridge. Seconds before they got there, it shattered into a thousand sparkling pieces, and they stared in horror as the crystal particles fell into the bottomless ravine.

Flores was close to tears. "How are we

going to get down?"

"Come on, there has to be another way," Gemma said in desperation, trying to keep her balance as the mountain shook with rage.

"The only way is over that narrow ledge," pointed Flores, her voice raised in panic.

"Let's go."

Gemma led the way, and together they clambered along the shaky ledge leading to the craggy rock face.

"There's nothing else for it – we'll have to take a chance and climb down here."

Hurriedly, they scrambled down the rock face, feeling their way desperately with their hands. The vibrations of the volcano caused stones and rubble to loosen and crumble beneath them.

"The mountain's falling apart," Flores shouted.

"Don't look down," Gemma warned her. "Hang on to the mountain and we'll be okay. Hurry, Flores, hurry!"

With only a short distance to go until they reached the bottom of the slope, Flores slipped, trapping her foot in a crevice.

"Help, I'm stuck!" she shouted.

Gemma climbed down until she was level with her, trying to avoid the falling debris which was raining down on them. With an almighty heave, she managed to pull Flores free and they both descended safely to the ground.

As the roaring of the volcano grew louder, red-hot lava spat into the sky then coursed in torrents down the outside of the volcano.

"Run!" screamed Gemma.

But Flores couldn't. Although her ankle wasn't badly hurt, she couldn't put her full weight on it. She limped a little way before falling to her knees in tears. "Go on – you go!" she cried, tears of frustration streaming down her face.

"I can't leave you..." Gemma panicked. Despairingly, Gemma turned around to see a magnificent white horse standing nearby. It was one of the wild horses which roamed the valley. It reared up on its hind legs and Gemma stared as it towered above her.

Shaking, she took the Gem Star from her pocket and thrust it at the horse. The dazzling light of the crystal seemed to tame the animal's fear. It stood still, snorting impatiently.

She hurried over and struggled to climb up on to the horse's strong, muscled back. It whinnied and tossed its head. Patting its mane, Gemma whispered, "Come on – you can help us!" and they galloped over to where Flores was.

The horse pawed impatiently at the ground, while Gemma dismounted and helped Flores up on to its back.

Minutes later, Gemma held on to the horse's long, silky white mane, with Flores tucked up behind gripping tightly around her waist.

"Hang on!" said Gemma, as they galloped furiously, outrunning the danger of the streaming lava. They rode like the wind back towards the city.

7. Pico Sees Clearly

With Gemma and Flores safely astride the white horse's back, they soon approached the edge of the Twin Lakes. Gemma could barely contain herself – she was so looking forward to seeing the expression on Pico's face when she handed him the Gem Star. As Gemma slid from the horse's back she gazed across at the far shore of the lake. She was so tired, she really couldn't face the rest of the journey back to the crystal cavern.

"You have done well, Gemma." The voice seemed to come from nowhere. Was she dreaming, or simply hearing things in her exhausted state? Then a hand rested gently on her shoulder. Pico!

Flores slid gently down from the horse, so as not to hurt her sprained ankle, and hugged Pico affectionately. She began chattering enthusiastically, telling him how she had met Gemma at the Sapphire Lake and how nasty Corvo and Velas had been.

As Gemma walked towards the wise old man, she looked into his pale blue eyes. She couldn't wait any longer to present Pico with the mystic crystal. "I have the Gem Star!" she cried eagerly, beaming with excitement.

"Thank you, Gemma," said Pico, taking the crystal from her and clasping it in his gnarled hands. "I thought that I would never see this again – you have been very brave. I hoped you would return safely, but my vision is growing weak and I could not be sure. Come inside..." He led them behind a rock, revealing a hidden entrance to the secret cavern. Putting his arm around Flores' shoulder, he helped her to hobble inside.

As he stared into the crystal, Pico's face lit up with sheer delight. "How strange it is to hold the Gem Star after all these years! It still glows as brightly as ever, and its energy is strong."

Wrapping it carefully in a piece of turquoise silk, he laid it down on the edge of the Pool of Destiny.

"I must summon the wise leaders," he said. "We have no time to waste. I want them to see the crystal – maybe then they will believe the truth."

"There is no need to summon us," resounded a clear, proud voice from behind them.

Turning around, Pico was amazed to see that the six leaders had come to seek his advice. Since the eruption of Fire Mountain the city was in a state of alarm, and they needed Pico's help.

"Everything will become clear when the Gem Star is returned to its rightful place," said Pico. He beckoned them to him. "Come – we will all see the truth together."

The leaders gathered around the Pool of Destiny.

"This is Gemma James," announced Pico, resting his hand in a grandfatherly way on her head. "Gemma has successfully completed the quest for the Gem Star, bringing this crystal safely back to our city."

She smiled nervously, looking at their long, flowing purple and gold robes.

Unwrapping the star, Pico cast it into the Pool of Destiny. As if by magic, the cavern lit up with a wonderful, mystical glow. Power and energy vibrated all around them, illuminating everything with a brilliant aura.

A rush of excitement charged through Gemma, and she smiled at Flores who was standing beside her. Nudging her friend, she whispered, "Wow! Isn't it amazing!"

The leaders stared eagerly into the water, gasping in astonishment as the future of Atlantis was reflected in their faces.

Solace, the oldest of the leaders, spoke up. "Pico's prediction is true," he said, sounding surprised and saddened.

"Atlantis is doomed to be destroyed."

Pico rallied them. "Heed this warning! Learn from it. Our fate lies with the future. We still have time to encourage our people to move away, to travel to other countries throughout the world. Our knowledge and our civilisation need not perish. This land may disappear into the sea, but we can survive elsewhere."

There was nodding and muttering, as the leaders listened to Pico's wise words. Then Solace spoke up once more. "Before we leave, can you tell us if the city is safe from Fire Mountain? Messengers report that the lava is flooding this way. Corvo and the boy Velas are said to be missing. They were last seen at the border of the Sapphire Lake near the Azure Forest."

Pico cast a ruby into the Pool of Destiny, and they all watched expectantly as another vision emerged.

"The city is safe – for the moment," announced Pico. "The lava flow will stop at the Twin Lakes."

"What about Corvo and Velas?" asked Gemma.

Pico shook his head solemnly. "I fear they have perished in the lava."

The leaders turned to leave the cavern and speak to their people about Fire Mountain. Now that Pico had proved that his predictions were true, there was much planning and preparation to be done. Solace was the last to leave.

Giving Gemma one last smile of gratitude, he turned and walked away.

Pico rested his hand on Gemma's shoulder. "Later, I will explain to Solace and the others who you are. They are wise enough to understand."

"Look!" exclaimed Flores, pointing at the vision within the Pool of Destiny. "The water is on fire!"

"No," said Pico. "Do not worry, it is merely an image of the everlasting flame of Atlantis – a sign that the Gem Star has restored the energy within the Pool of Destiny."

His words triggered Gemma's memory. "The lady in the jewellery shop mentioned the everlasting flame," she countered.

"Which lady?" asked Flores.

"From the future – she sells jewellery in the Azores, and she told me about the mysterious Lake of Fire which shines in the dark with a fiery red glow."

"There is no Lake of Fire in Atlantis," said Pico.

"But she said the lake was set within the crater of an ancient volcano that was extinguished many years ago," recalled Gemma.

Pico looked thoughtful. "Perhaps it is the crater of Fire Mountain."

"What else did the woman from the future say?" Flores asked.

"She told me that the lake was sparkling and clear during the day, but at sunset it glowed as if it were on fire. According to legend, the fiery glow is the everlasting flame of Atlantis – a reminder that the past is forever a part of the future."

Pico smiled kindly at Gemma. "How very true. It took a girl from the future to help us right the past."

"I never thought of it like that," she said wistfully. "But I suppose time really doesn't matter. When I return to the future, not a second will have passed since I left. Nothing will have changed."

"Do you have to go back?" asked Flores sadly.

Gemma sighed. "I wish I could stay longer, but the power of the magic jewellery only lasts for a short time. I'll have to go soon."

"What's the future like?" said Flores, fascinated.

Gemma pondered for a moment. "Well, it's a mixture of everything that has happened throughout history. Each era and civilisation is layered on top of the next, influencing how we live."

"I suppose as time passes, legends and facts become muddled until no one knows the truth," suggested Pico.

"Well, the mysteries and myths of Atlantis are safe with me," Gemma reassured him. "Besides, no one would believe me – the lost continent of Atlantis is one of the most famous legends of our time."

"I cannot thank you enough," said Pico.

"And I wish you didn't have to leave," echoed Flores.

"Well," said Gemma. "I'm glad I was able to help. The quest for the Gem Star has been an amazing adventure for me, but I'm afraid it's time for me to leave."

"I'd like you to keep my magic necklace, as a token of our friendship," she said to Flores.

"I wish you luck and good fortune, Gemma," said Pico, smiling warmly.

With that simple exchange of words, Gemma unfastened the necklace's clasp. The whole world seemed to spin around, faster and faster, and Gemma felt as if she was falling. Then, with a bump, she landed back on the floor in her hotel room in the Azores.

Sunlight was pouring through the bay windows, and everything was just the way she had left it. No time had passed. A warm sea breeze wafted in through the open doors leading to the veranda.

Gazing out at the Azores, Gemma felt as if she was looking at the past through the eyes of the future. The Twin Lakes sparkled in the distance.

Suddenly she remembered something important.

"Oh my goodness – the map!"

She had forgotten to give it to Pico – it was still in the pocket of her jeans. She pulled it out, noticing how the parchment had yellowed with age to a deep amber shade and how the brightly-coloured markings had faded.

She was just about to fold it carefully and place it safely in her jewellery box, when she noticed one final message written on the ancient map.

Gemma read it and smiled.

The Gem Star quest has been completed.
All of the obstacles are now defeated.
Gaze back in time and you will see,
The part you played in history.